Suzanne Downey Farrell grew up in Pennsylvania and is one of six children. She attended Delaware County Community College, where she obtained an associate's degree in business management. She now resides in Florida with her husband, Jack. Time spent reading to her two sons was a major influence for writing children's books. Their enthusiasm and enjoyment were her inspiration.

ELLA BELLA
Loves the Rain

Written By:
Suzanne Downey Farrell

Illustrated By:
Mary Kratz

AUSTIN MACAULEY PUBLISHERS™
LONDON • CAMBRIDGE • NEW YORK • SHARJAH

A CIP catalogue record for this title is available from the British Library.

ISBN 9781528990677 (Paperback)
ISBN 9781528990684 (ePub e-book)

www.austinmacauley.com

First Published (2020)
Austin Macauley Publishers Ltd
25 Canada Square
Canary Wharf
London
E14 5LQ

This book is dedicated to an adorable child named Anthony Meo, a very precious child who, at the age of three, stands up and sings a song which silences a room. His love of life is contagious.

Ella Bella looks out
from her window pane,

looking for the first
drops of rain.

The ___ is cloudy, dark and heavy.

Ella Bella is excited
to get ready.

Ella Bella puts her rain coat
and boots on,
so she can go outside before the
rain is gone.

This is such
fun for
Ella Bella,
as she
listens
to the
raindrops
hit her
umbrella.

Ella Bella jumps
from puddle to puddle,

Where lots of leaves were
gathered in a huddle.

A skip, a jump
and
in a

Flash.

Ella Bella
makes a
BIG! splash.

All the birds and
bugs stay inside,
Ella Bella knows
where they hide.

Ella Bella watches the showers,
as they fall on all the flowers.

The rain has slowed to a drip,
Ella Bella will now enjoy a skip.

Ella Bella watches the sky
put on a beautiful show.
From behind the clouds
comes a rainbow!

Yes, Ella Bella loves the rain.

CPSIA information can be obtained
at www.ICGtesting.com
Printed in the USA
BVHW020750011120
592280BV00026B/1627